W9-AUJ-109

Nearing the end of World War Two, Captain America and Bucky were tasked with guarding an experimental remote-controlled drone bomber. The drone was booby-trapped, however, and in the subsequent explosion Bucky was killed and Cap was thrown into the ocean below-- where he would stay in suspended animation until he was discovered by the modern-day Avengers!

Upon waking, Captain America found himself in an America that was not his own. When the Avengers disappeared, a confused and increasingly desperate Cap struck out on his own to discover the truth...and wound up being shot by a young girl he was trying to assist.

After waking up in the hospital, a very delusional Captain America meets Rick Jones, a young man with ties to the Avengers. The two of them pair up to get to the bottom of the Avengers' disappearance: A being from space has turned them to stone. With the Avengers restored, the now lucid Cap turns his attention to his next step, getting back to his own time!

CAPTAIN AMERICA:
MAN OUT OF TIME, PART 3

Mark Waid – Writer
Jorge Molina – Breakdowns
Karl Kesel & Scott Hanna – Finishes
Frank D'Armata – Colorist
VC's Joe Sabino – Letterer & Production
Bryan Hitch, Paul Neary & Paul Mounts – Cover Art
Lauren Sankovitch – Associate Editor
Tom Brevoort – Editor
Joe Quesada – Editor in Chief
Dan Buckley – Publisher
Alan Fine – Executive Producer

MAI 848 7060

visit us at www.abdopublishing.com

Reinforced library bound edition published in 2012 by Spotlight, a division of the ABDO Group, 8000 West 78th Street, Edina, Minnesota 55439. Spotlight produces high-quality reinforced library bound editions for schools and libraries. Published by agreement with Marvel Entertainment, LLC. The stories, characters, and incidents mentioned are entirely fictional. All rights reserved. Used under authorization.

Printed in the United States of America, Melrose Park, Illinois.
052011
092011
 This book contains at least 10% recycled materials.

Library of Congress Cataloging-in-Publication Data

Waid, Mark.
  Man out of time / writer, Mark Waid ; penciler, Jorge Molina.
    v. cm.
  Summary: Frozen in suspended animation for over sixty years, World War II superhero Captain America, aka Steve Rogers, wakes up in the twenty-first century and must adapt to a very changed world.
  ISBN 978-1-59961-936-1 (v. 1) -- ISBN 978-1-59961-937-8 (v. 2) -- ISBN 978-1-59961-938-5 (v. 3) -- ISBN 978-1-59961-939-2 (v. 4) -- ISBN 978-1-59961-940-8 (v. 5)
  1. Graphic novels. [1. Graphic novels. 2. Superheroes--Fiction. 3. Space and time--Fiction.] I. Molina, Jorge, 1984- ill. II. Title.
  PZ7.7.W35Man 2011
  741.5'973--dc22
                            2011013320

All Spotlight books are reinforced library bindings
and manufactured in the United States of America.

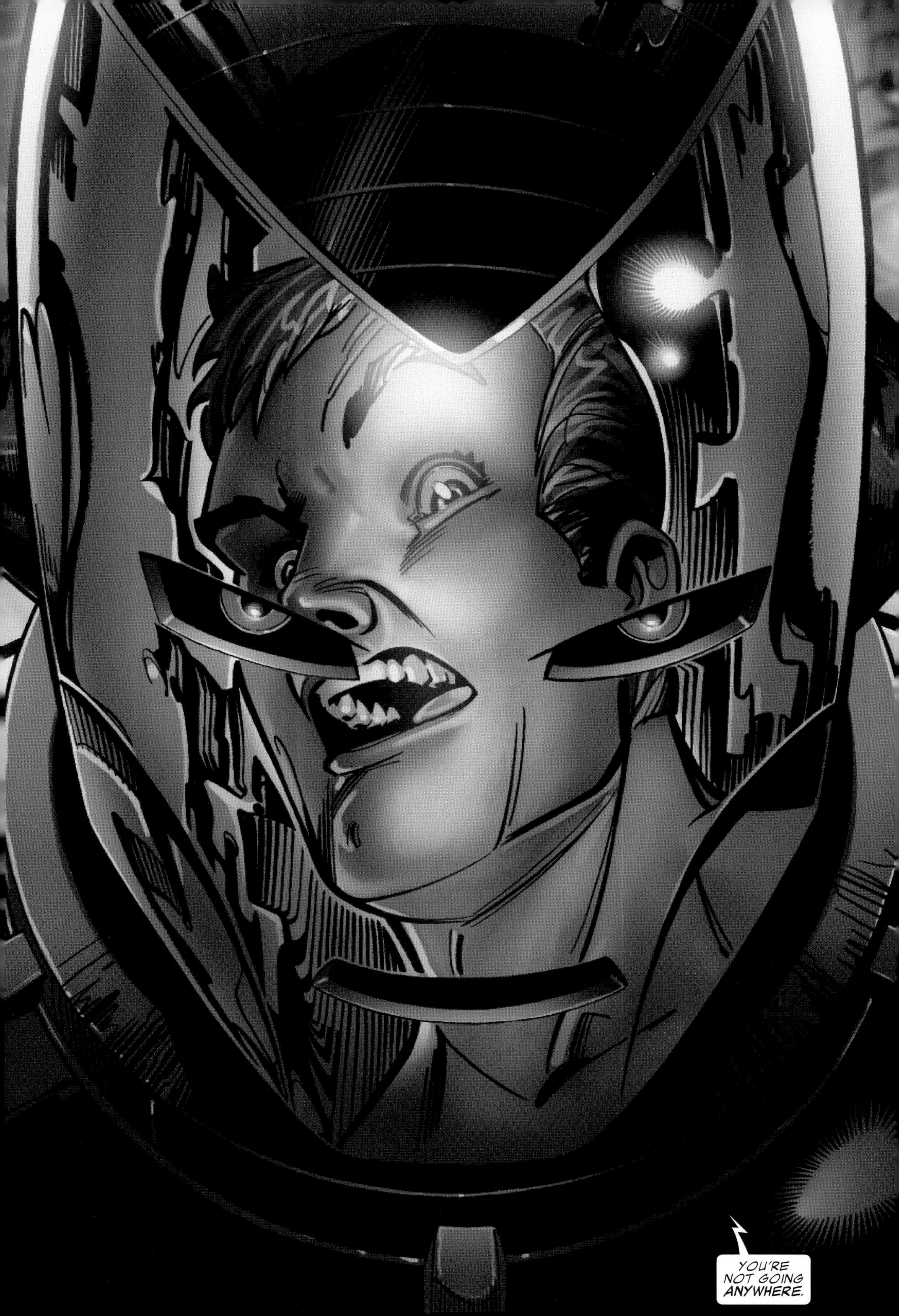
YOU'RE NOT GOING ANYWHERE.

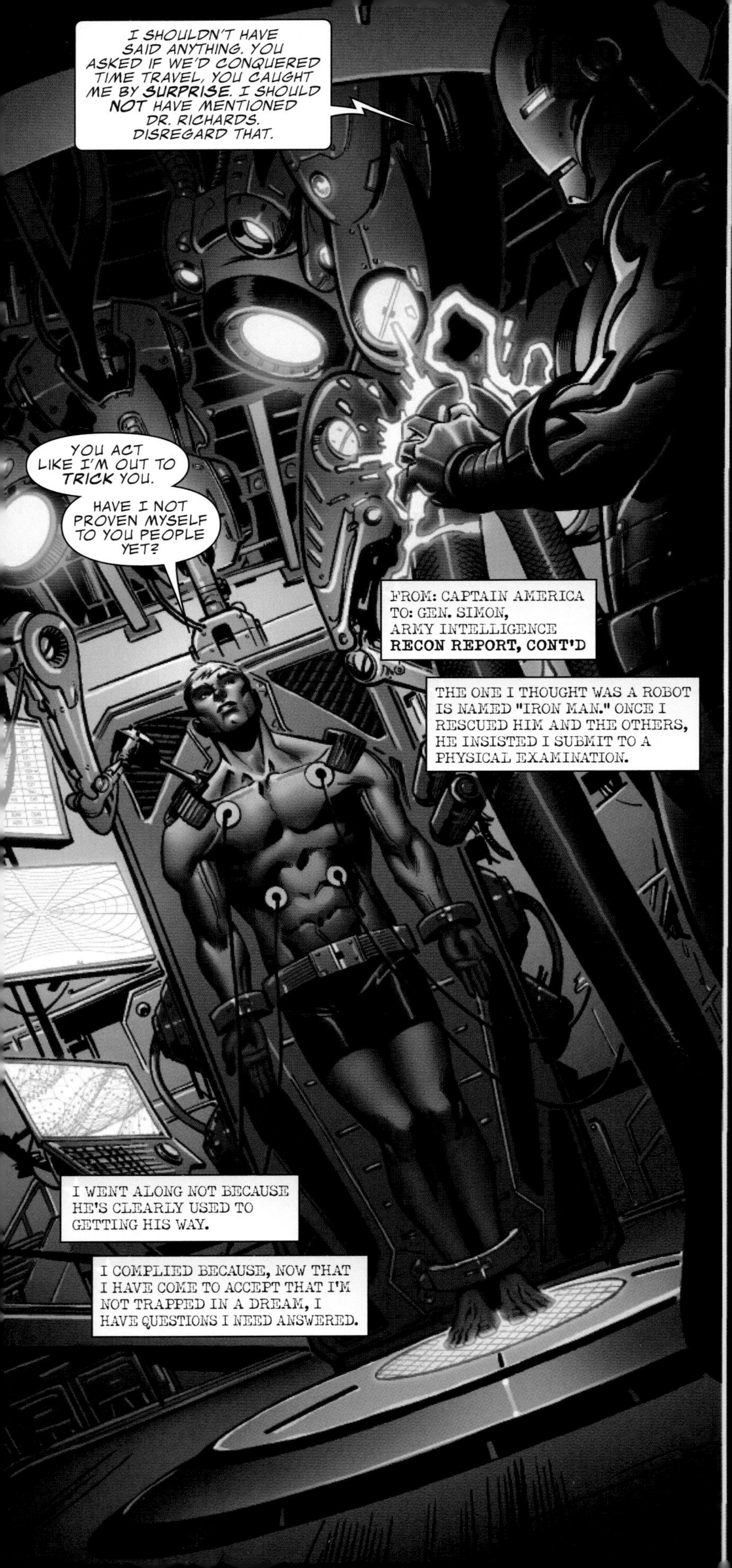
I SHOULDN'T HAVE SAID ANYTHING. YOU ASKED IF WE'D CONQUERED TIME TRAVEL, YOU CAUGHT ME BY SURPRISE. I SHOULD NOT HAVE MENTIONED DR. RICHARDS. DISREGARD THAT.
YOU ACT LIKE I'M OUT TO TRICK YOU.
HAVE I NOT PROVEN MYSELF TO YOU PEOPLE YET?
FROM: CAPTAIN AMERICA TO: GEN. SIMON, ARMY INTELLIGENCE RECON REPORT, CONT'D
THE ONE I THOUGHT WAS A ROBOT IS NAMED "IRON MAN." ONCE I RESCUED HIM AND THE OTHERS, HE INSISTED I SUBMIT TO A PHYSICAL EXAMINATION.
I WENT ALONG NOT BECAUSE HE'S CLEARLY USED TO GETTING HIS WAY.
I COMPLIED BECAUSE, NOW THAT I HAVE COME TO ACCEPT THAT I'M NOT TRAPPED IN A DREAM, I HAVE QUESTIONS I NEED ANSWERED.

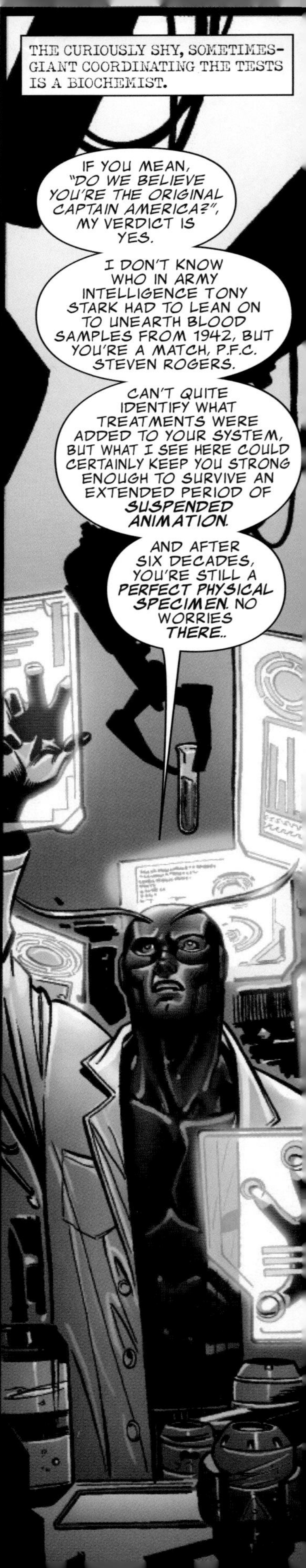
THE CURIOUSLY SHY, SOMETIMES-GIANT COORDINATING THE TESTS IS A BIOCHEMIST.
IF YOU MEAN, "DO WE BELIEVE YOU'RE THE ORIGINAL CAPTAIN AMERICA?", MY VERDICT IS YES.
I DON'T KNOW WHO IN ARMY INTELLIGENCE TONY STARK HAD TO LEAN ON TO UNEARTH BLOOD SAMPLES FROM 1942, BUT YOU'RE A MATCH, P.F.C. STEVEN ROGERS.
CAN'T QUITE IDENTIFY WHAT TREATMENTS WERE ADDED TO YOUR SYSTEM, BUT WHAT I SEE HERE COULD CERTAINLY KEEP YOU STRONG ENOUGH TO SURVIVE AN EXTENDED PERIOD OF SUSPENDED ANIMATION.
AND AFTER SIX DECADES, YOU'RE STILL A PERFECT PHYSICAL SPECIMEN. NO WORRIES THERE..

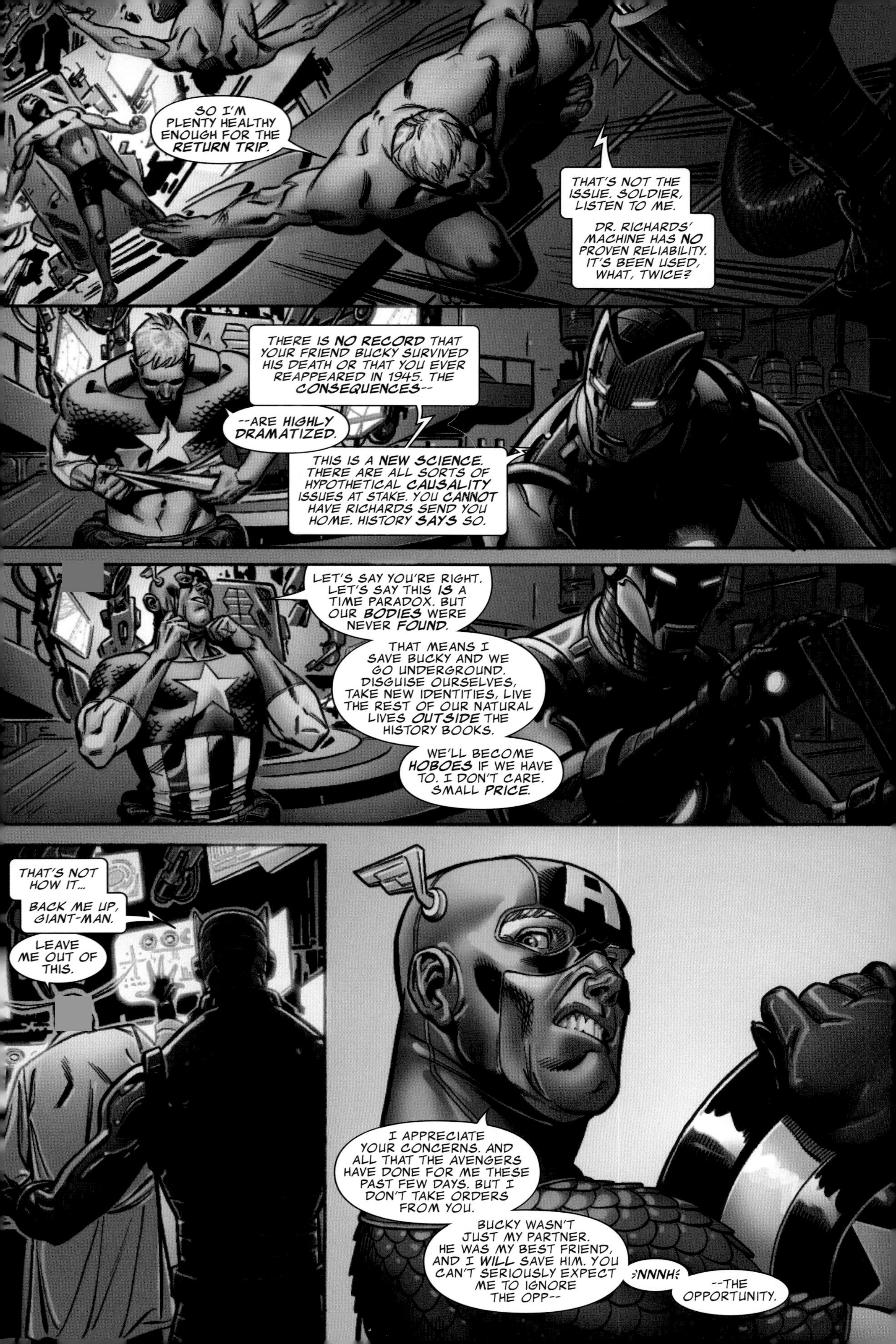

SO I'M PLENTY HEALTHY ENOUGH FOR THE RETURN TRIP.
THAT'S NOT THE ISSUE. SOLDIER, LISTEN TO ME.
DR. RICHARDS' MACHINE HAS NO PROVEN RELIABILITY. IT'S BEEN USED, WHAT, TWICE?
THERE IS NO RECORD THAT YOUR FRIEND BUCKY SURVIVED HIS DEATH OR THAT YOU EVER REAPPEARED IN 1945. THE CONSEQUENCES--
--ARE HIGHLY DRAMATIZED.
THIS IS A NEW SCIENCE. THERE ARE ALL SORTS OF HYPOTHETICAL CAUSALITY ISSUES AT STAKE. YOU CANNOT HAVE RICHARDS SEND YOU HOME. HISTORY SAYS SO.
LET'S SAY YOU'RE RIGHT. LET'S SAY THIS IS A TIME PARADOX. BUT OUR BODIES WERE NEVER FOUND.
THAT MEANS I SAVE BUCKY AND WE GO UNDERGROUND. DISGUISE OURSELVES, TAKE NEW IDENTITIES, LIVE THE REST OF OUR NATURAL LIVES OUTSIDE THE HISTORY BOOKS.
WE'LL BECOME HOBOES IF WE HAVE TO. I DON'T CARE. SMALL PRICE.
THAT'S NOT HOW IT...
BACK ME UP, GIANT-MAN.
LEAVE ME OUT OF THIS.
I APPRECIATE YOUR CONCERNS. AND ALL THAT THE AVENGERS HAVE DONE FOR ME THESE PAST FEW DAYS. BUT I DON'T TAKE ORDERS FROM YOU.
BUCKY WASN'T JUST MY PARTNER. HE WAS MY BEST FRIEND, AND I WILL SAVE HIM. YOU CAN'T SERIOUSLY EXPECT ME TO IGNORE THE OPP--
NNNH
--THE OPPORTUNITY.

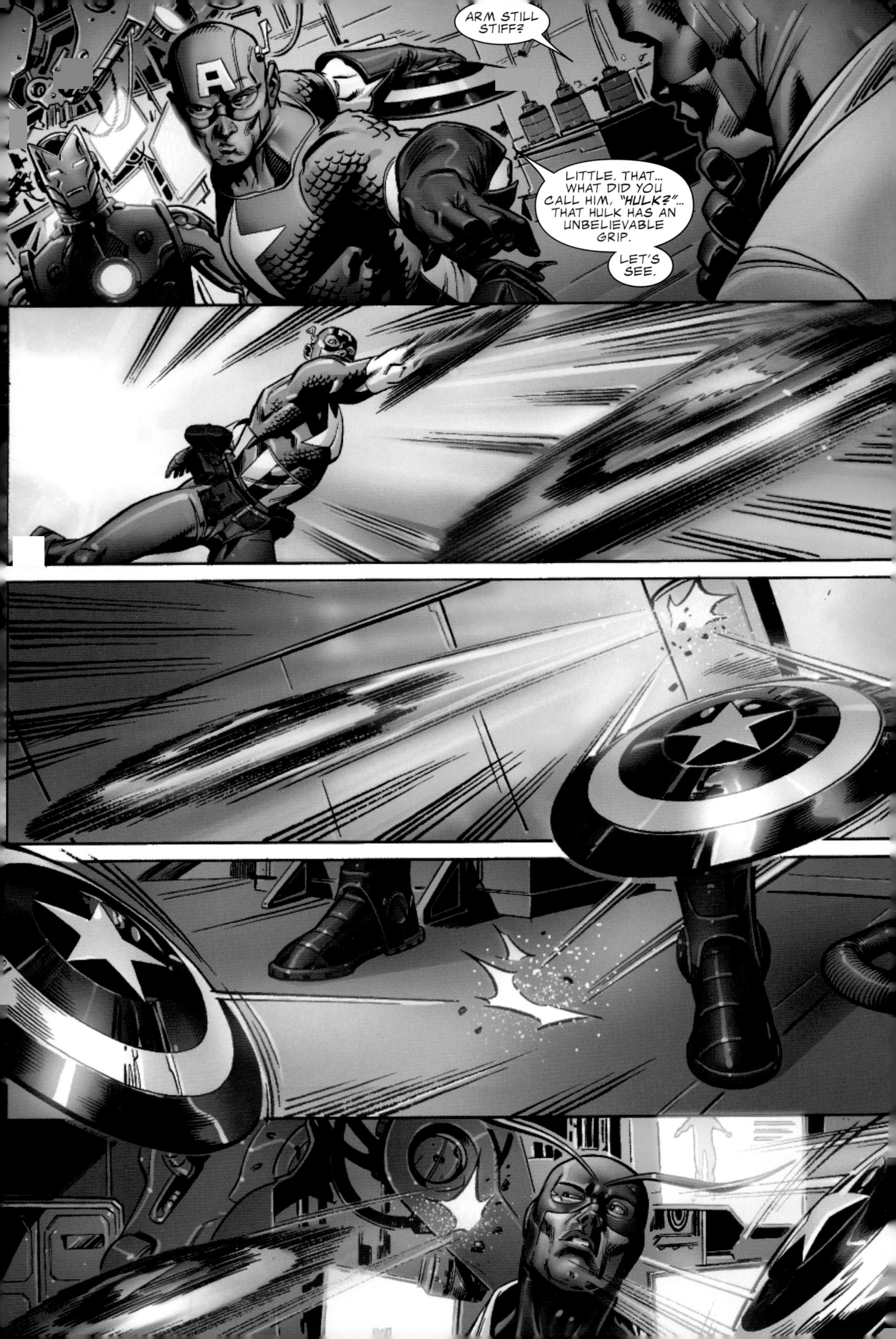
ARM STILL STIFF?
LITTLE. THAT... WHAT DID YOU CALL HIM, "HULK?"... THAT HULK HAS AN UNBELIEVABLE GRIP.
LET'S SEE.

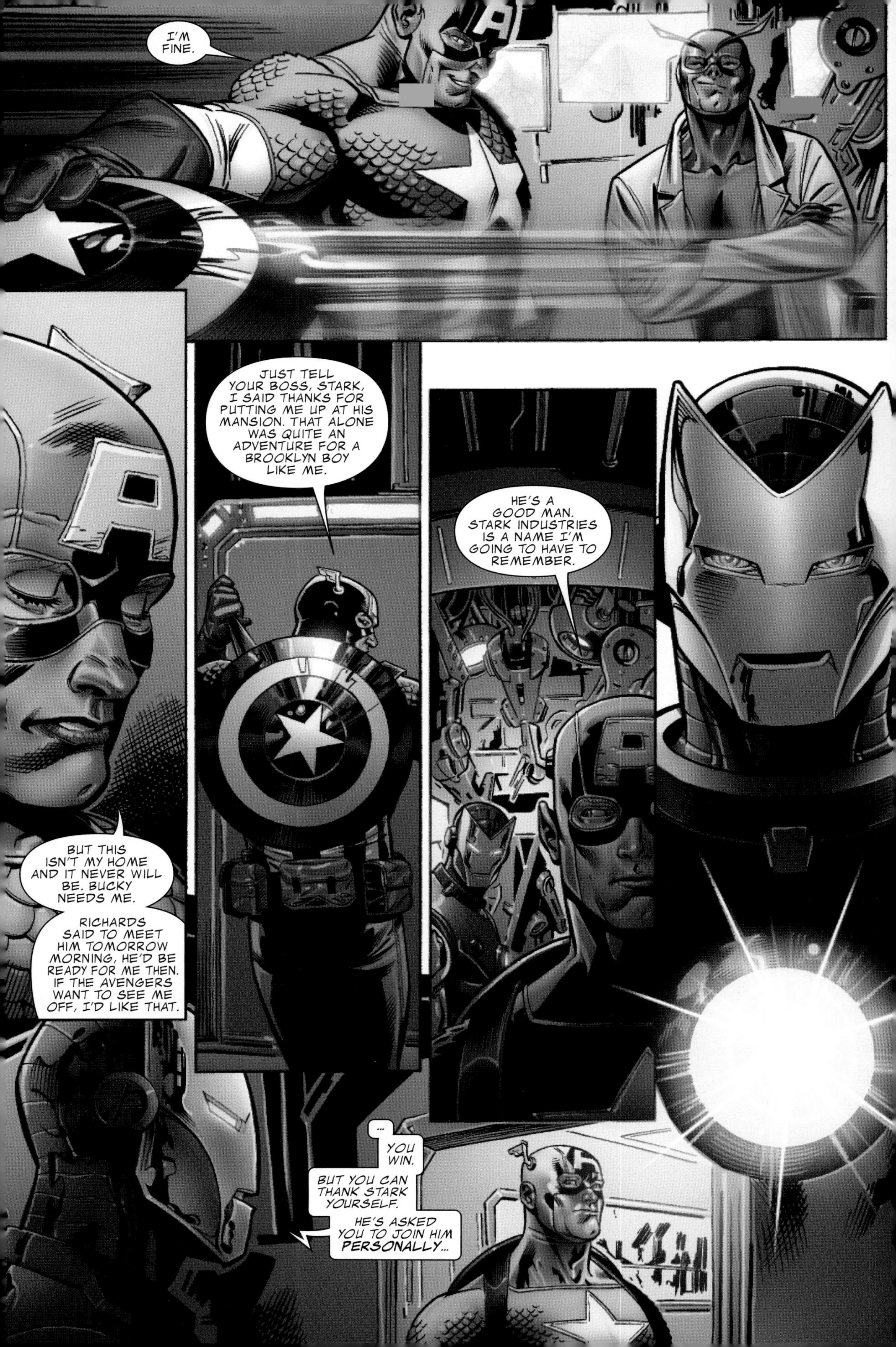
I'M FINE.
JUST TELL YOUR BOSS, STARK, I SAID THANKS FOR PUTTING ME UP AT HIS MANSION. THAT ALONE WAS QUITE AN ADVENTURE FOR A BROOKLYN BOY LIKE ME.
HE'S A GOOD MAN. STARK INDUSTRIES IS A NAME I'M GOING TO HAVE TO REMEMBER.
BUT THIS ISN'T MY HOME AND IT NEVER WILL BE. BUCKY NEEDS ME.
RICHARDS SAID TO MEET HIM TOMORROW MORNING, HE'D BE READY FOR ME THEN. IF THE AVENGERS WANT TO SEE ME OFF, I'D LIKE THAT.
...
YOU WIN.
BUT YOU CAN THANK STARK YOURSELF.
HE'S ASKED YOU TO JOIN HIM **PERSONALLY**...

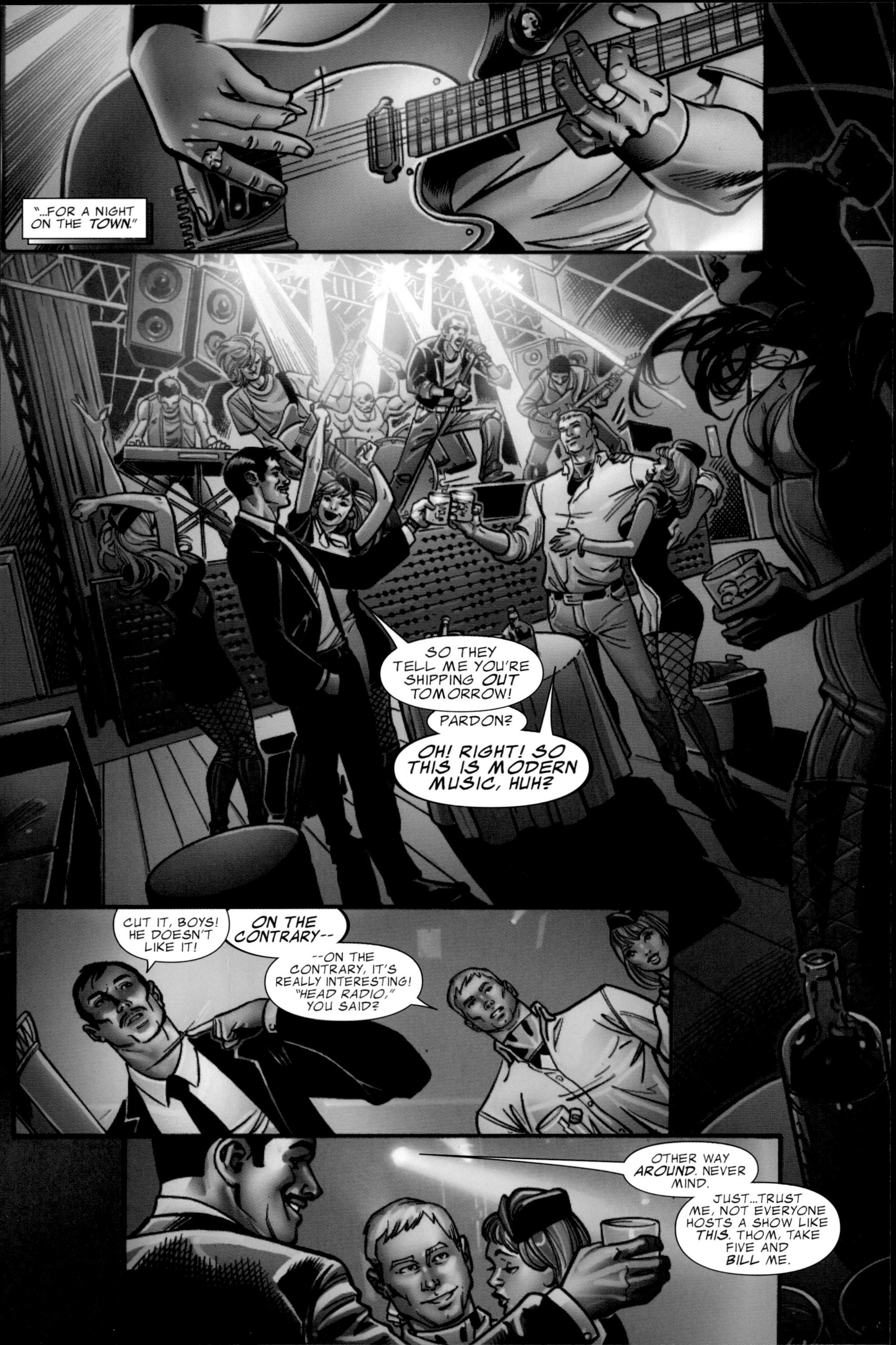
"...FOR A NIGHT ON THE TOWN."
SO THEY TELL ME YOU'RE SHIPPING OUT TOMORROW!
PARDON?
OH! RIGHT! SO THIS IS MODERN MUSIC, HUH?
CUT IT, BOYS! HE DOESN'T LIKE IT!
ON THE CONTRARY--
--ON THE CONTRARY, IT'S REALLY INTERESTING! "HEAD RADIO," YOU SAID?
OTHER WAY AROUND. NEVER MIND.
JUST...TRUST ME, NOT EVERYONE HOSTS A SHOW LIKE THIS. THOM, TAKE FIVE AND BILL ME.

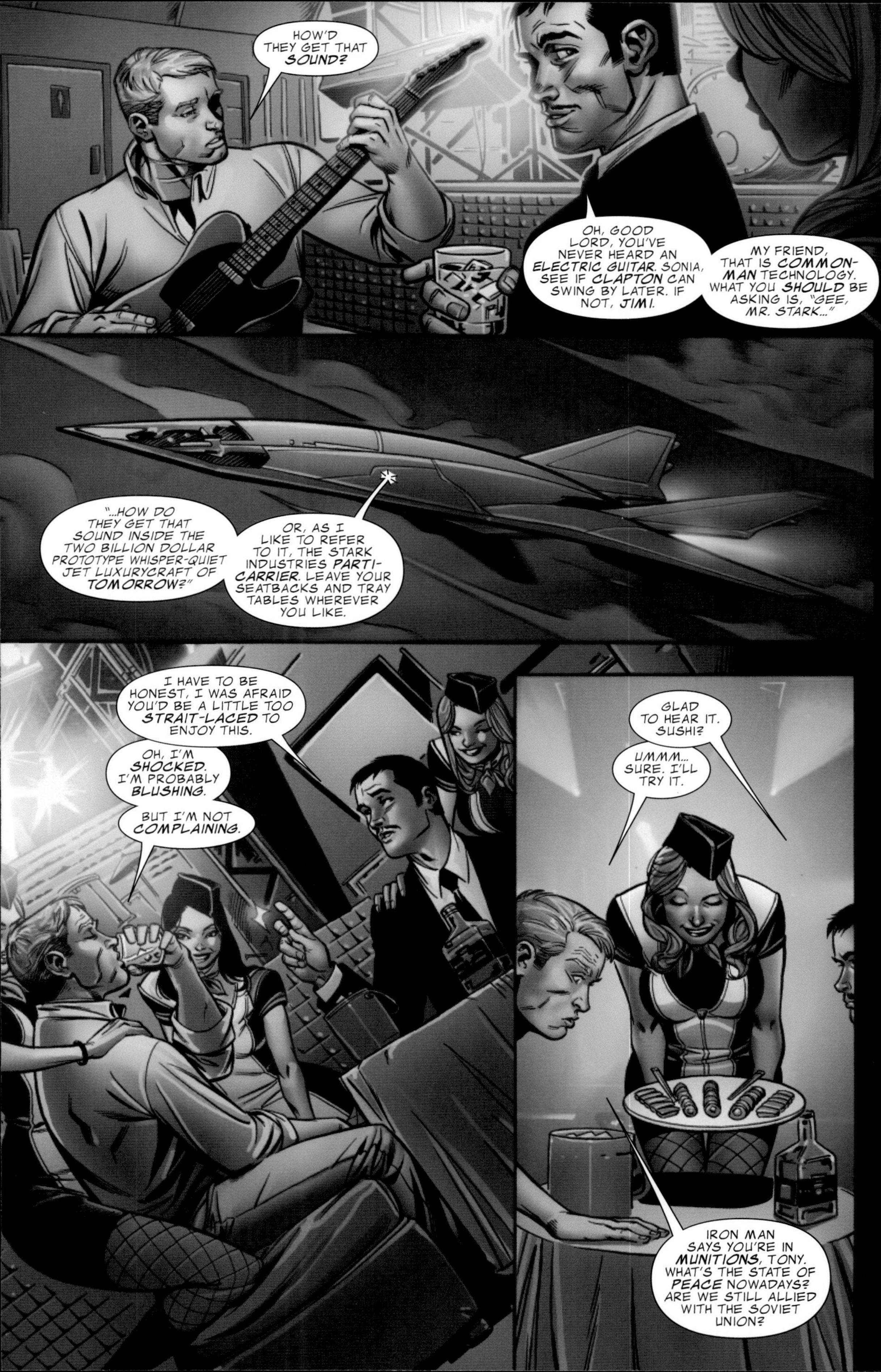
HOW'D THEY GET THAT SOUND?
OH, GOOD LORD, YOU'VE NEVER HEARD AN ELECTRIC GUITAR. SONIA, SEE IF CLAPTON CAN SWING BY LATER. IF NOT, JIMI.
MY FRIEND, THAT IS COMMON-MAN TECHNOLOGY. WHAT YOU SHOULD BE ASKING IS, "GEE, MR. STARK...
"...HOW DO THEY GET THAT SOUND INSIDE THE TWO BILLION DOLLAR PROTOTYPE WHISPER-QUIET JET LUXURYCRAFT OF TOMORROW?"
OR, AS I LIKE TO REFER TO IT, THE STARK INDUSTRIES PARTI-CARRIER. LEAVE YOUR SEATBACKS AND TRAY TABLES WHEREVER YOU LIKE.
I HAVE TO BE HONEST, I WAS AFRAID YOU'D BE A LITTLE TOO STRAIT-LACED TO ENJOY THIS.
OH, I'M SHOCKED. I'M PROBABLY BLUSHING.
BUT I'M NOT COMPLAINING.
GLAD TO HEAR IT. SUSHI?
UMMM... SURE. I'LL TRY IT.
IRON MAN SAYS YOU'RE IN MUNITIONS, TONY. WHAT'S THE STATE OF PEACE NOWADAYS? ARE WE STILL ALLIED WITH THE SOVIET UNION?

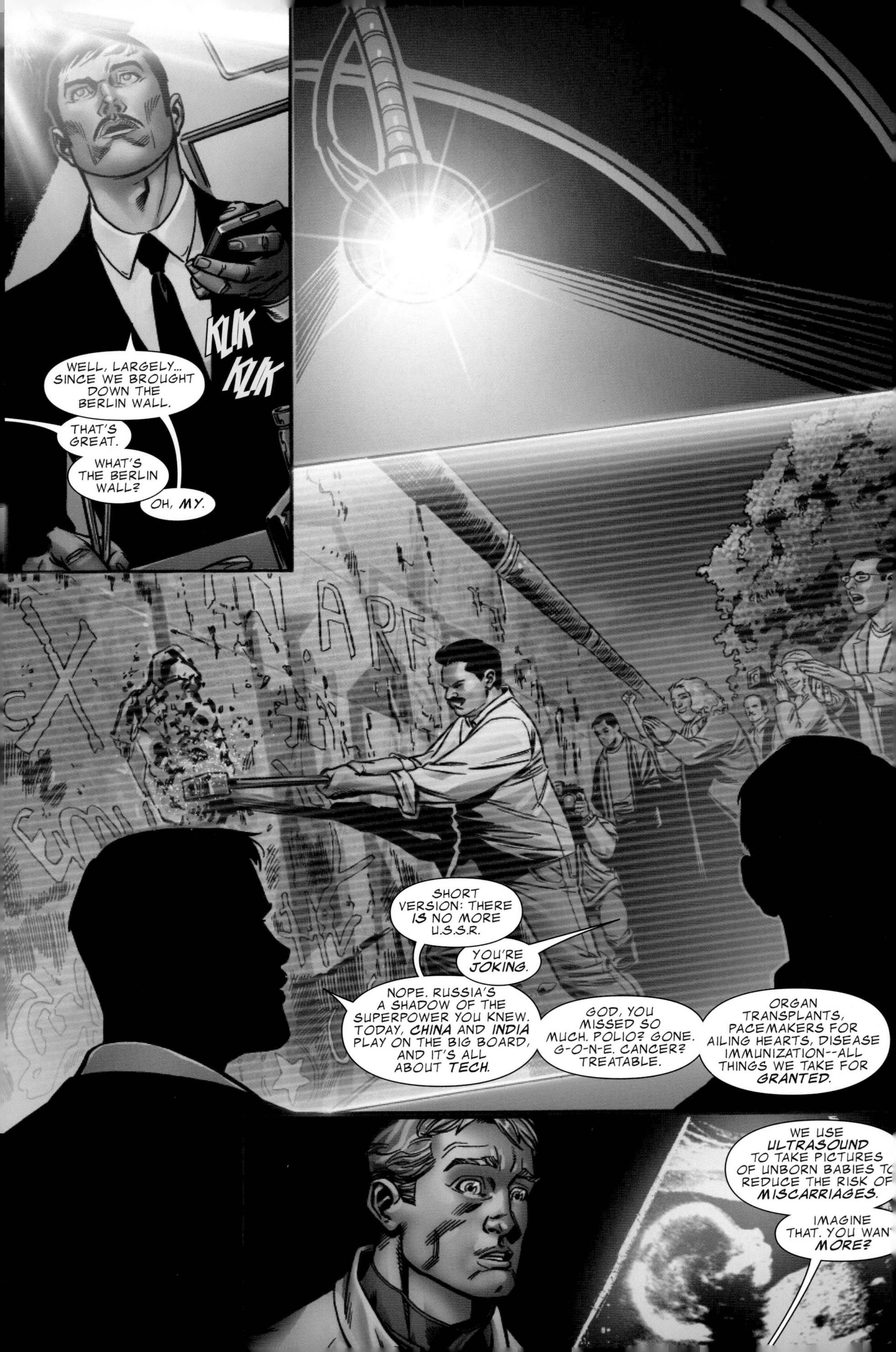

KLIK KLIK
WELL, LARGELY... SINCE WE BROUGHT DOWN THE BERLIN WALL.
THAT'S GREAT.
WHAT'S THE BERLIN WALL?
OH, MY.
SHORT VERSION: THERE IS NO MORE U.S.S.R.
YOU'RE JOKING.
NOPE. RUSSIA'S A SHADOW OF THE SUPERPOWER YOU KNEW. TODAY, CHINA AND INDIA PLAY ON THE BIG BOARD, AND IT'S ALL ABOUT TECH.
GOD, YOU MISSED SO MUCH. POLIO? GONE. G-O-N-E. CANCER? TREATABLE.
ORGAN TRANSPLANTS, PACEMAKERS FOR AILING HEARTS, DISEASE IMMUNIZATION--ALL THINGS WE TAKE FOR GRANTED.
WE USE ULTRASOUND TO TAKE PICTURES OF UNBORN BABIES TO REDUCE THE RISK OF MISCARRIAGES.
IMAGINE THAT. YOU WANT MORE?

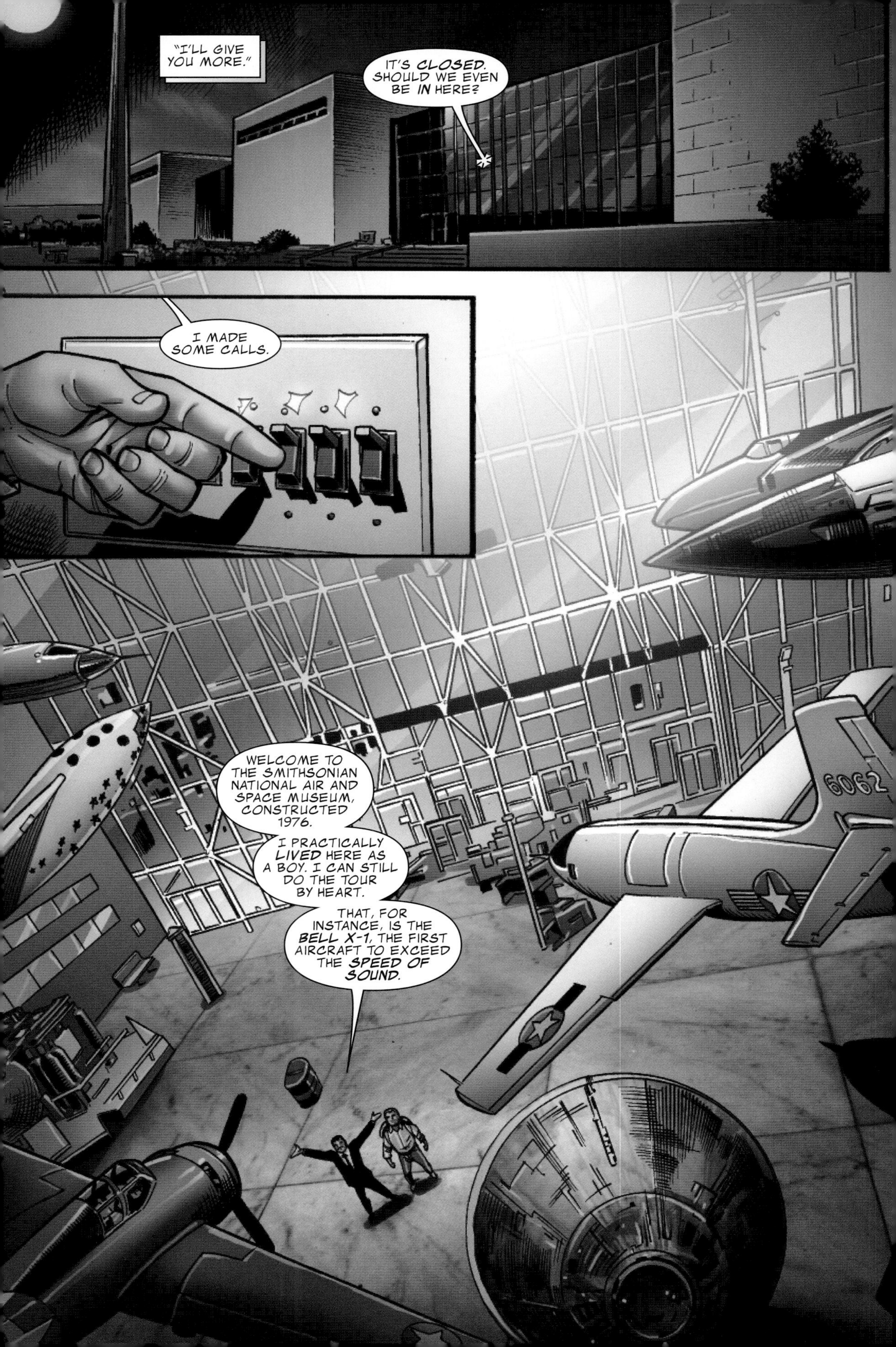
"I'LL GIVE YOU MORE."
IT'S CLOSED. SHOULD WE EVEN BE IN HERE?
I MADE SOME CALLS.
WELCOME TO THE SMITHSONIAN NATIONAL AIR AND SPACE MUSEUM, CONSTRUCTED 1976.
I PRACTICALLY LIVED HERE AS A BOY. I CAN STILL DO THE TOUR BY HEART.
THAT, FOR INSTANCE, IS THE BELL X-1, THE FIRST AIRCRAFT TO EXCEED THE SPEED OF SOUND.
6062

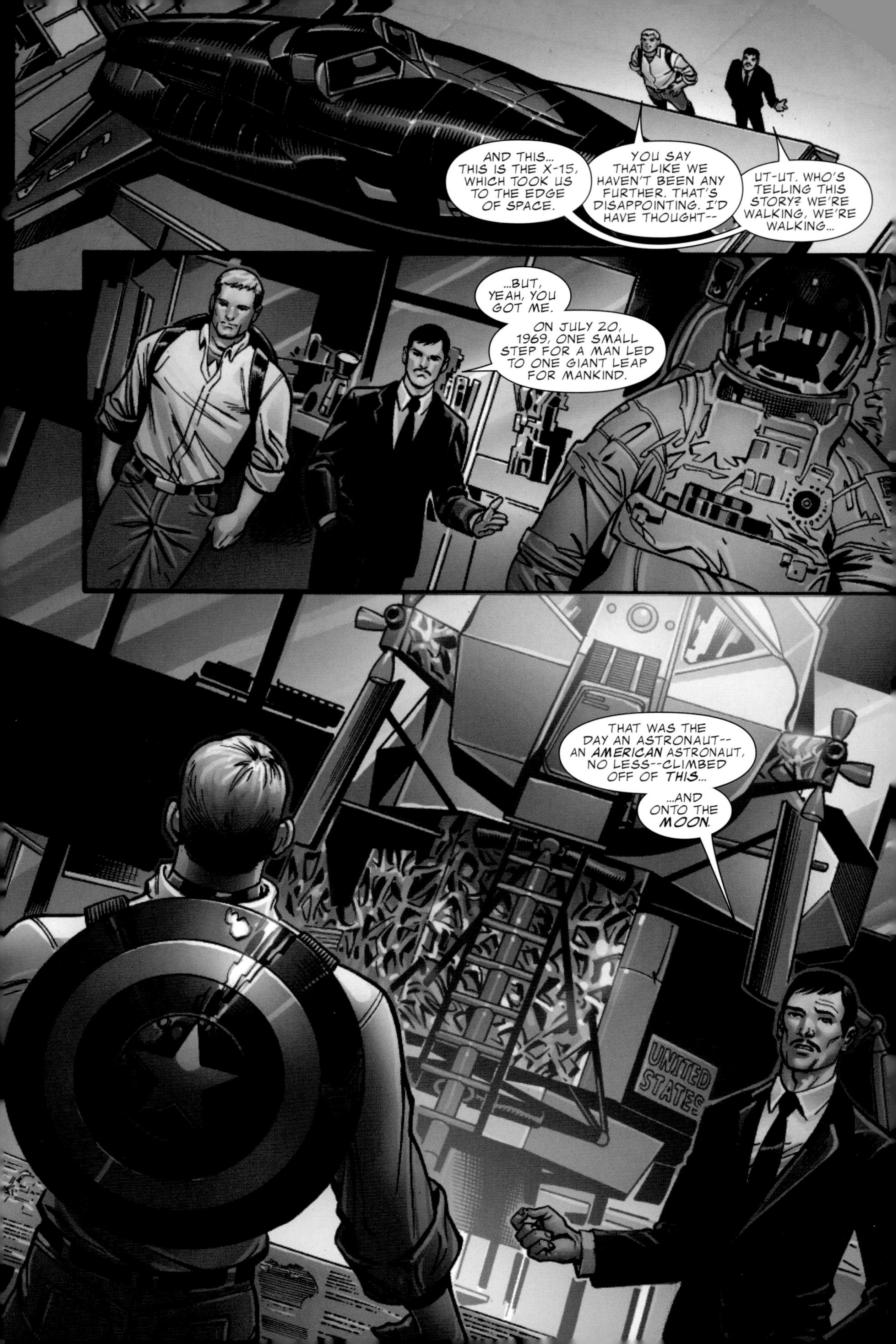
AND THIS... THIS IS THE X-15, WHICH TOOK US TO THE EDGE OF SPACE.
YOU SAY THAT LIKE WE HAVEN'T BEEN ANY FURTHER. THAT'S DISAPPOINTING. I'D HAVE THOUGHT--
UT-UT. WHO'S TELLING THIS STORY? WE'RE WALKING, WE'RE WALKING...
...BUT, YEAH, YOU GOT ME.
ON JULY 20, 1969, ONE SMALL STEP FOR A MAN LED TO ONE GIANT LEAP FOR MANKIND.
THAT WAS THE DAY AN ASTRONAUT-- AN *AMERICAN* ASTRONAUT, NO LESS--CLIMBED OFF OF *THIS*...
...AND ONTO THE *MOON*.
UNITED STATES

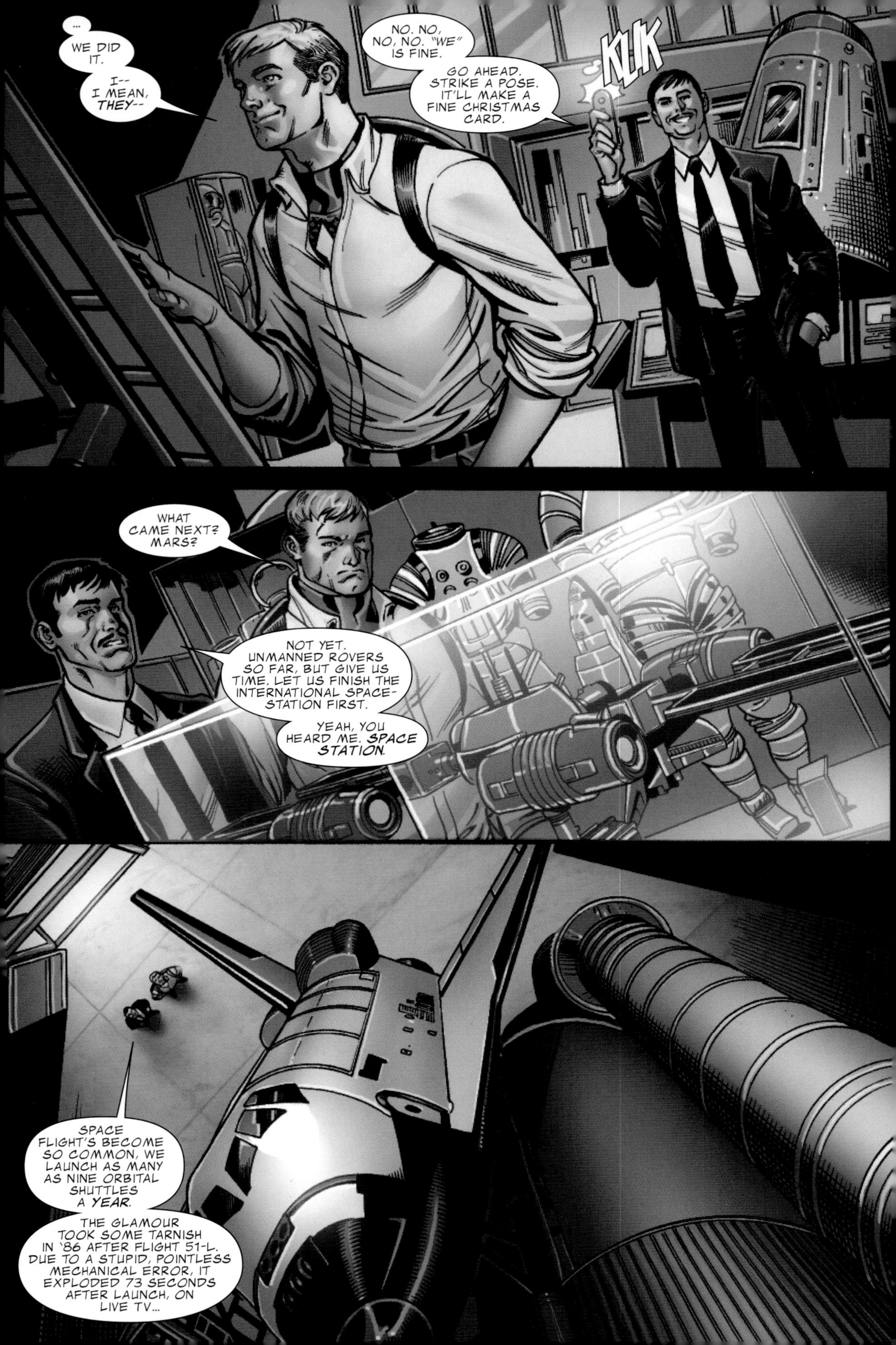
...
WE DID IT.
I-- I MEAN, THEY--
NO. NO, NO, NO. "WE" IS FINE.
KLIK
GO AHEAD. STRIKE A POSE. IT'LL MAKE A FINE CHRISTMAS CARD.
WHAT CAME NEXT? MARS?
NOT YET. UNMANNED ROVERS SO FAR, BUT GIVE US TIME. LET US FINISH THE INTERNATIONAL SPACE-STATION FIRST.
YEAH, YOU HEARD ME. SPACE STATION.
SPACE FLIGHT'S BECOME SO COMMON, WE LAUNCH AS MANY AS NINE ORBITAL SHUTTLES A YEAR.
THE GLAMOUR TOOK SOME TARNISH IN '86 AFTER FLIGHT 51-L. DUE TO A STUPID, POINTLESS MECHANICAL ERROR, IT EXPLODED 73 SECONDS AFTER LAUNCH, ON LIVE TV...

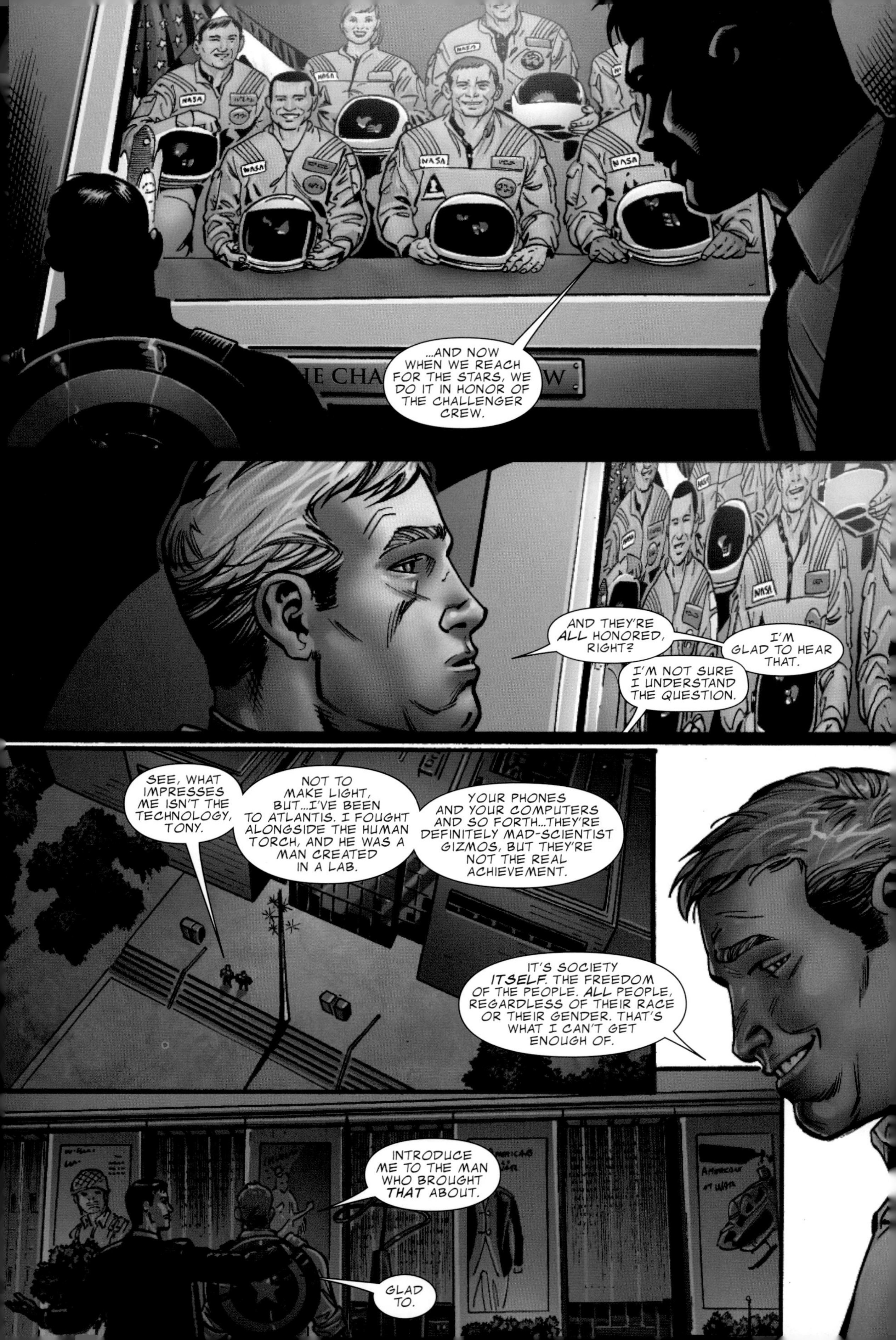
...AND NOW WHEN WE REACH FOR THE STARS, WE DO IT IN HONOR OF THE CHALLENGER CREW.
AND THEY'RE ALL HONORED, RIGHT?
I'M NOT SURE I UNDERSTAND THE QUESTION.
I'M GLAD TO HEAR THAT.
SEE, WHAT IMPRESSES ME ISN'T THE TECHNOLOGY, TONY.
NOT TO MAKE LIGHT, BUT...I'VE BEEN TO ATLANTIS. I FOUGHT ALONGSIDE THE HUMAN TORCH, AND HE WAS A MAN CREATED IN A LAB.
YOUR PHONES AND YOUR COMPUTERS AND SO FORTH...THEY'RE DEFINITELY MAD-SCIENTIST GIZMOS, BUT THEY'RE NOT THE REAL ACHIEVEMENT.
IT'S SOCIETY ITSELF. THE FREEDOM OF THE PEOPLE. ALL PEOPLE, REGARDLESS OF THEIR RACE OR THEIR GENDER. THAT'S WHAT I CAN'T GET ENOUGH OF.
INTRODUCE ME TO THE MAN WHO BROUGHT THAT ABOUT.
GLAD TO.

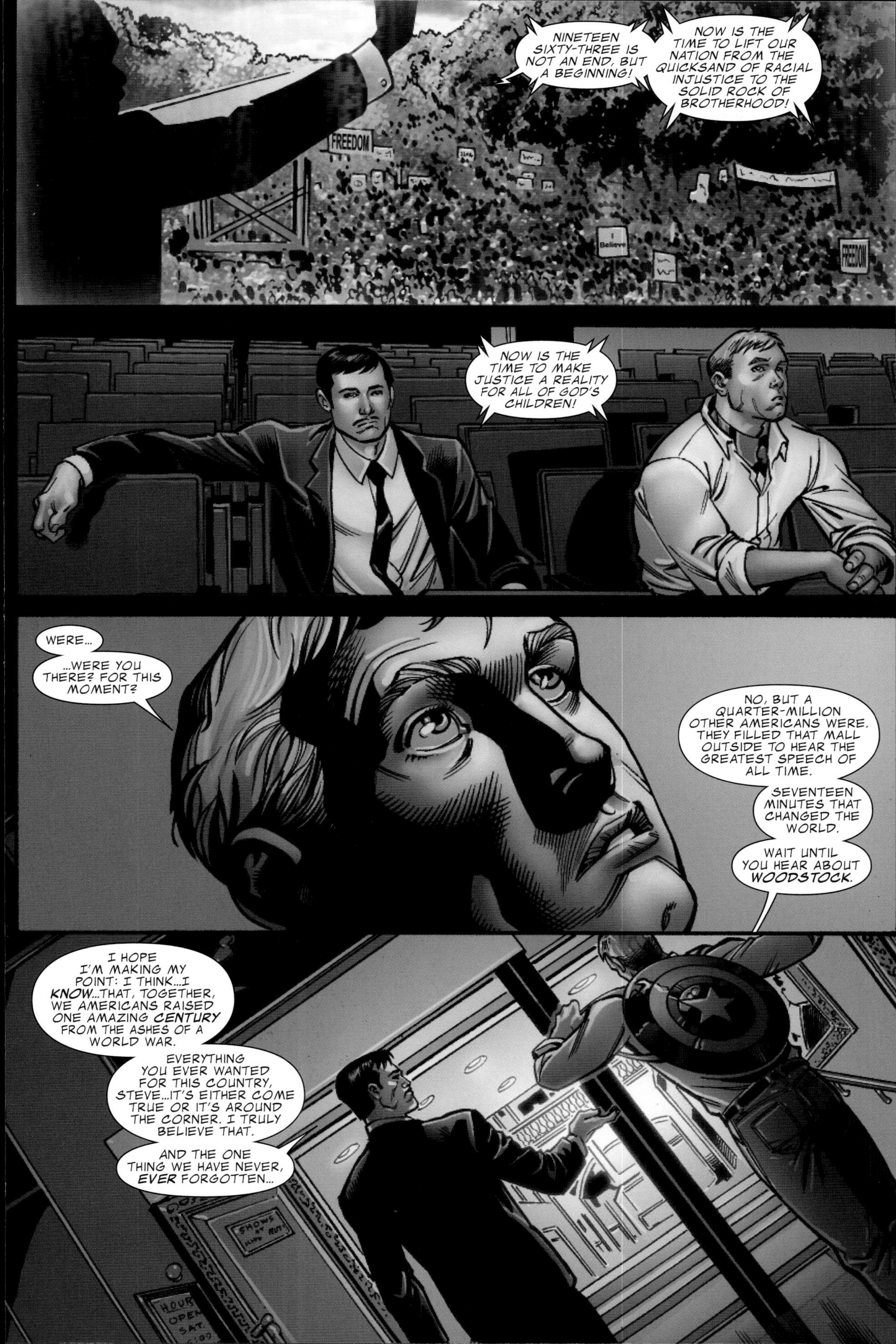

NINETEEN SIXTY-THREE IS NOT AN END, BUT A BEGINNING!
NOW IS THE TIME TO LIFT OUR NATION FROM THE QUICKSAND OF RACIAL INJUSTICE TO THE SOLID ROCK OF BROTHERHOOD!
FREEDOM
I Believe
FREEDOM
NOW IS THE TIME TO MAKE JUSTICE A REALITY FOR ALL OF GOD'S CHILDREN!
WERE...
...WERE YOU THERE? FOR THIS MOMENT?
NO, BUT A QUARTER-MILLION OTHER AMERICANS WERE. THEY FILLED THAT MALL OUTSIDE TO HEAR THE GREATEST SPEECH OF ALL TIME.
SEVENTEEN MINUTES THAT CHANGED THE WORLD.
WAIT UNTIL YOU HEAR ABOUT WOODSTOCK.
I HOPE I'M MAKING MY POINT: I THINK...I KNOW...THAT, TOGETHER, WE AMERICANS RAISED ONE AMAZING CENTURY FROM THE ASHES OF A WORLD WAR.
EVERYTHING YOU EVER WANTED FOR THIS COUNTRY, STEVE...IT'S EITHER COME TRUE OR IT'S AROUND THE CORNER. I TRULY BELIEVE THAT.
AND THE ONE THING WE HAVE NEVER, EVER FORGOTTEN...

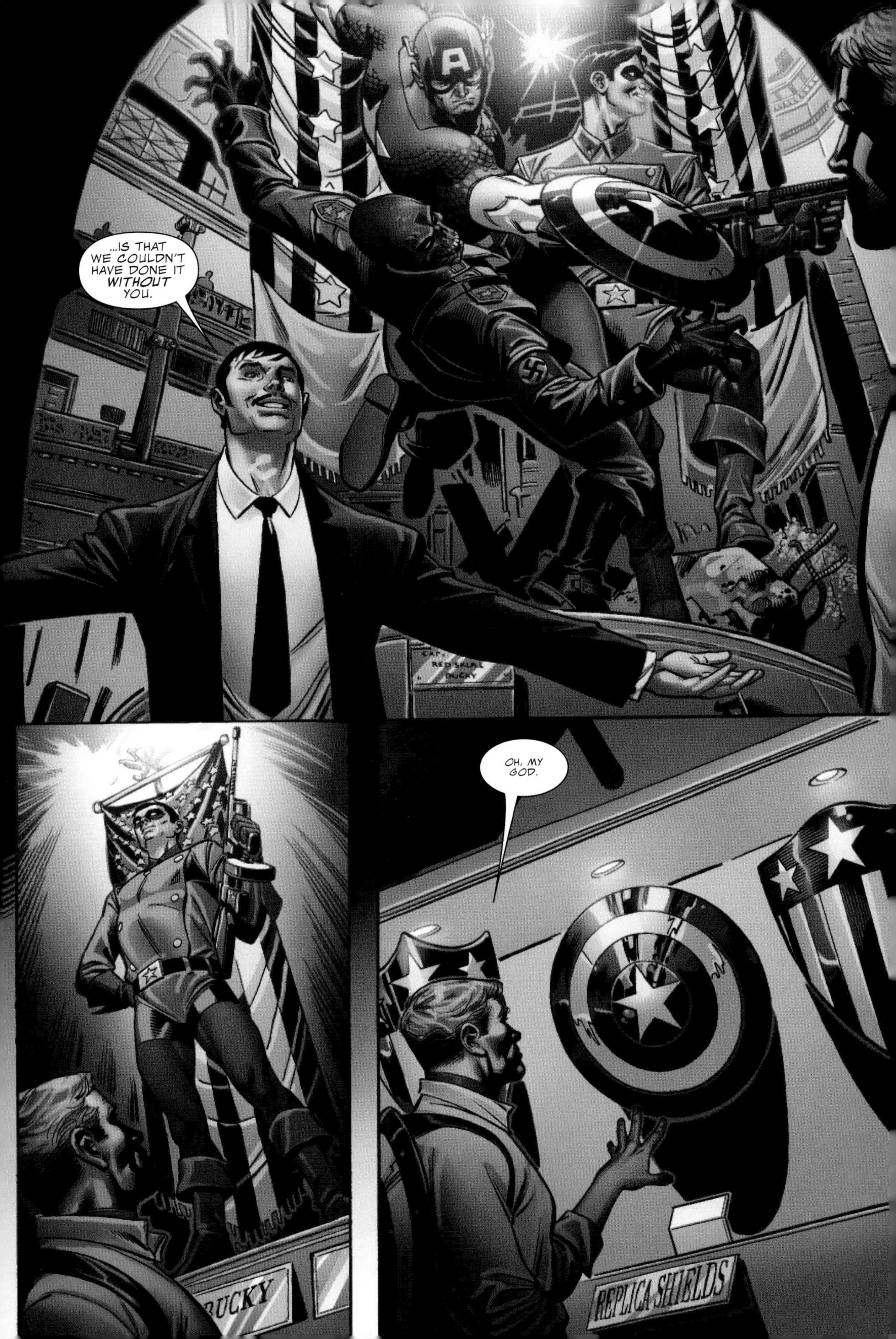
...IS THAT WE COULDN'T HAVE DONE IT *WITHOUT* YOU.
BUCKY
OH, MY GOD.
REPLICA SHIELDS

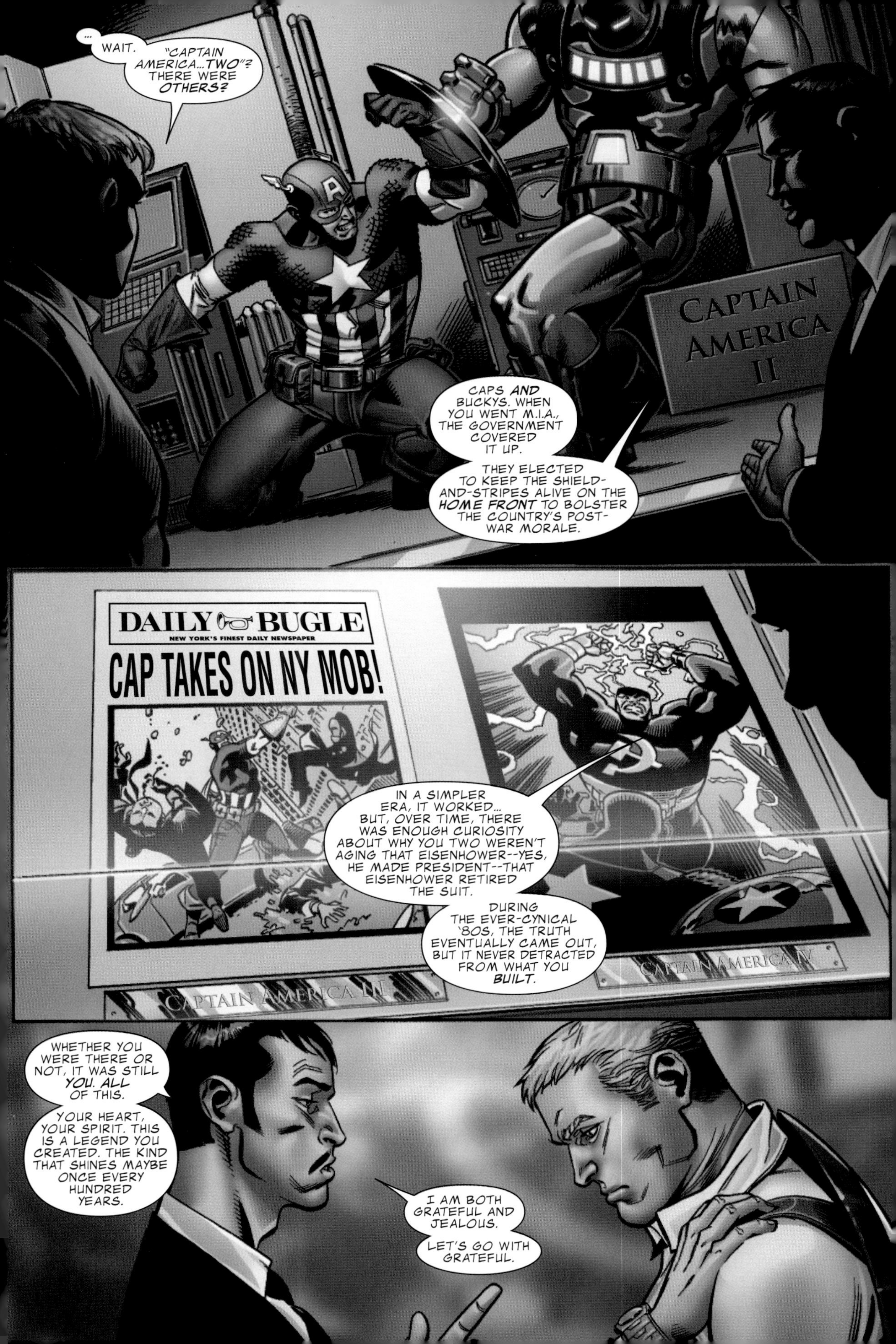

...
WAIT.
"CAPTAIN AMERICA...TWO"? THERE WERE OTHERS?
CAPTAIN AMERICA II
CAPS AND BUCKYS. WHEN YOU WENT M.I.A., THE GOVERNMENT COVERED IT UP.
THEY ELECTED TO KEEP THE SHIELD-AND-STRIPES ALIVE ON THE HOME FRONT TO BOLSTER THE COUNTRY'S POST-WAR MORALE.
DAILY BUGLE
NEW YORK'S FINEST DAILY NEWSPAPER
CAP TAKES ON NY MOB!
IN A SIMPLER ERA, IT WORKED... BUT, OVER TIME, THERE WAS ENOUGH CURIOSITY ABOUT WHY YOU TWO WEREN'T AGING THAT EISENHOWER--YES, HE MADE PRESIDENT--THAT EISENHOWER RETIRED THE SUIT.
DURING THE EVER-CYNICAL '80S, THE TRUTH EVENTUALLY CAME OUT, BUT IT NEVER DETRACTED FROM WHAT YOU BUILT.
CAPTAIN AMERICA III
CAPTAIN AMERICA IV
WHETHER YOU WERE THERE OR NOT, IT WAS STILL YOU. ALL OF THIS.
YOUR HEART, YOUR SPIRIT. THIS IS A LEGEND YOU CREATED. THE KIND THAT SHINES MAYBE ONCE EVERY HUNDRED YEARS.
I AM BOTH GRATEFUL AND JEALOUS.
LET'S GO WITH GRATEFUL.

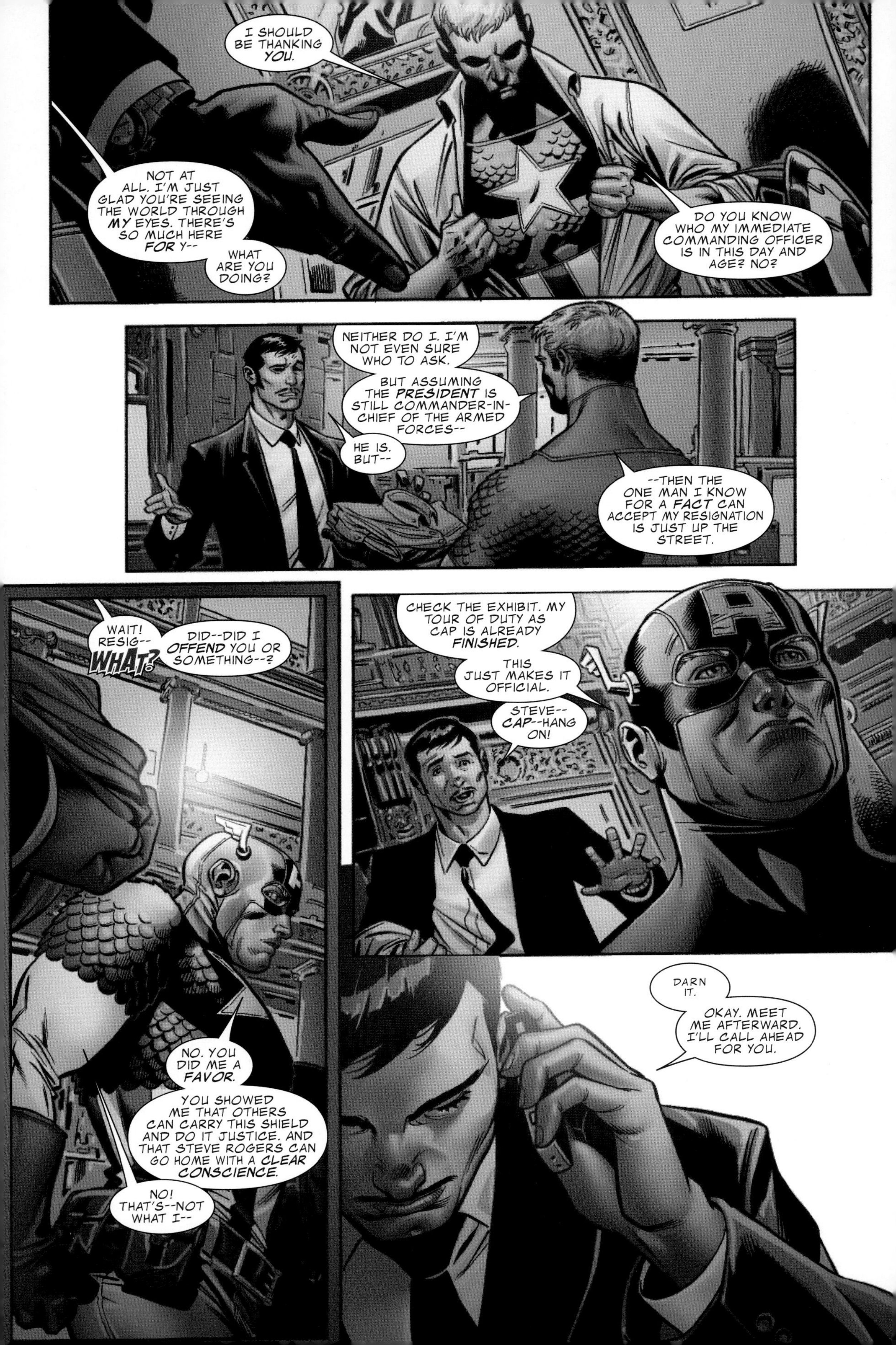
I SHOULD BE THANKING YOU.
NOT AT ALL. I'M JUST GLAD YOU'RE SEEING THE WORLD THROUGH MY EYES. THERE'S SO MUCH HERE FOR Y--
WHAT ARE YOU DOING?
DO YOU KNOW WHO MY IMMEDIATE COMMANDING OFFICER IS IN THIS DAY AND AGE? NO?
NEITHER DO I. I'M NOT EVEN SURE WHO TO ASK.
BUT ASSUMING THE PRESIDENT IS STILL COMMANDER-IN-CHIEF OF THE ARMED FORCES--
HE IS. BUT--
--THEN THE ONE MAN I KNOW FOR A FACT CAN ACCEPT MY RESIGNATION IS JUST UP THE STREET.
WAIT! RESIG--WHAT?
DID--DID I OFFEND YOU OR SOMETHING--?
NO. YOU DID ME A FAVOR.
YOU SHOWED ME THAT OTHERS CAN CARRY THIS SHIELD AND DO IT JUSTICE. AND THAT STEVE ROGERS CAN GO HOME WITH A CLEAR CONSCIENCE.
NO! THAT'S--NOT WHAT I--
CHECK THE EXHIBIT. MY TOUR OF DUTY AS CAP IS ALREADY FINISHED.
THIS JUST MAKES IT OFFICIAL.
STEVE--CAP--HANG ON!
DARN IT.
OKAY. MEET ME AFTERWARD. I'LL CALL AHEAD FOR YOU.

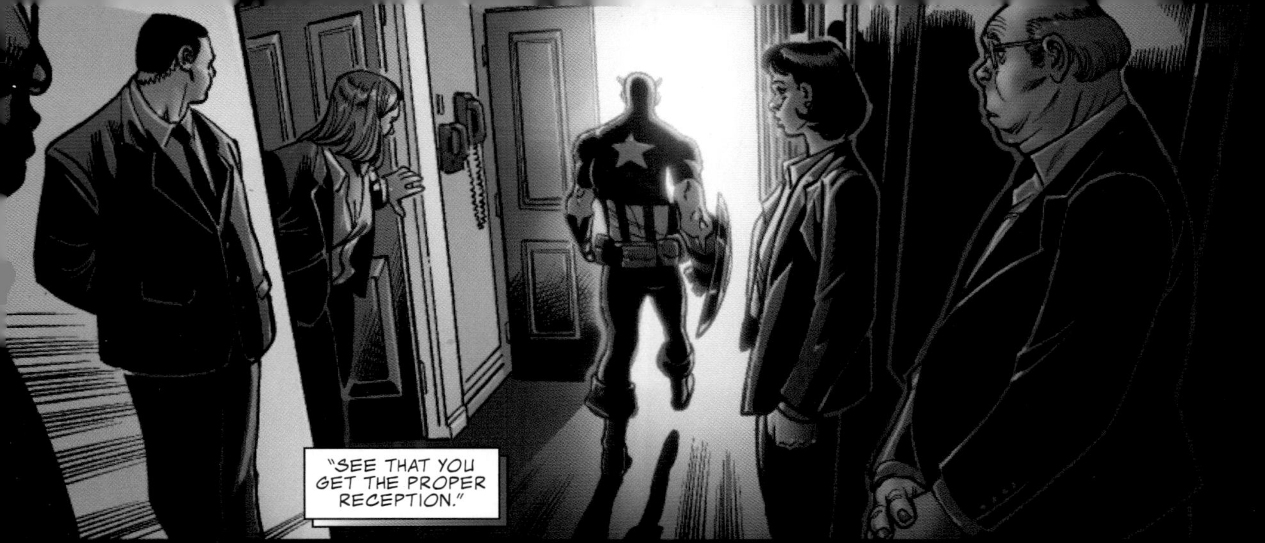
"SEE THAT YOU GET THE PROPER RECEPTION."

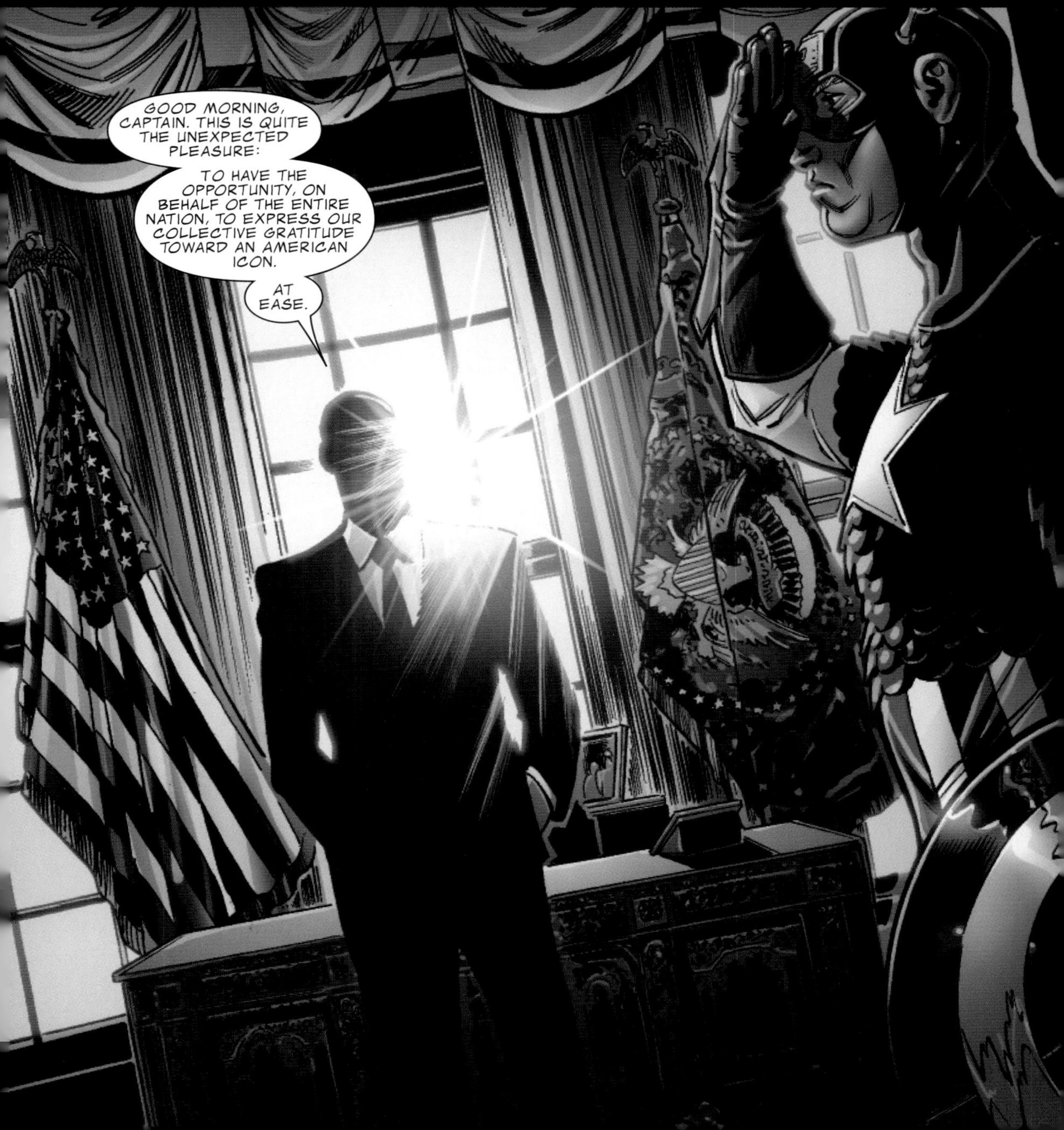
GOOD MORNING, CAPTAIN. THIS IS QUITE THE UNEXPECTED PLEASURE:
TO HAVE THE OPPORTUNITY, ON BEHALF OF THE ENTIRE NATION, TO EXPRESS OUR COLLECTIVE GRATITUDE TOWARD AN AMERICAN ICON.
AT EASE.

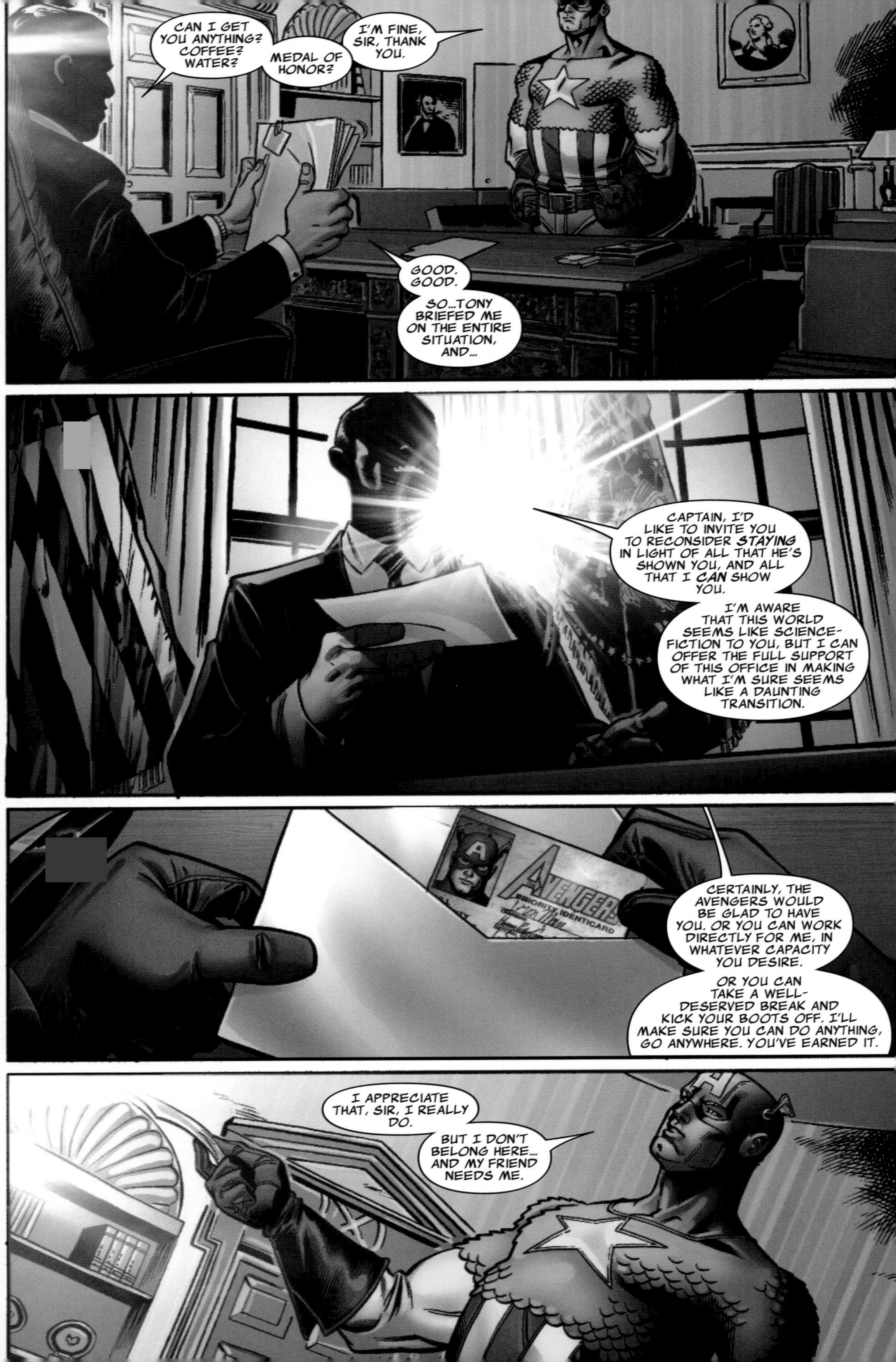
CAN I GET YOU ANYTHING? COFFEE? WATER?
MEDAL OF HONOR?
I'M FINE, SIR, THANK YOU.
GOOD. GOOD.
SO...TONY BRIEFED ME ON THE ENTIRE SITUATION, AND...
CAPTAIN, I'D LIKE TO INVITE YOU TO RECONSIDER STAYING IN LIGHT OF ALL THAT HE'S SHOWN YOU, AND ALL THAT I CAN SHOW YOU.
I'M AWARE THAT THIS WORLD SEEMS LIKE SCIENCE-FICTION TO YOU, BUT I CAN OFFER THE FULL SUPPORT OF THIS OFFICE IN MAKING WHAT I'M SURE SEEMS LIKE A DAUNTING TRANSITION.
AVENGERS
PRIORITY IDENTICARD
CERTAINLY, THE AVENGERS WOULD BE GLAD TO HAVE YOU. OR YOU CAN WORK DIRECTLY FOR ME, IN WHATEVER CAPACITY YOU DESIRE.
OR YOU CAN TAKE A WELL-DESERVED BREAK AND KICK YOUR BOOTS OFF. I'LL MAKE SURE YOU CAN DO ANYTHING, GO ANYWHERE. YOU'VE EARNED IT.
I APPRECIATE THAT, SIR, I REALLY DO.
BUT I DON'T BELONG HERE... AND MY FRIEND NEEDS ME.

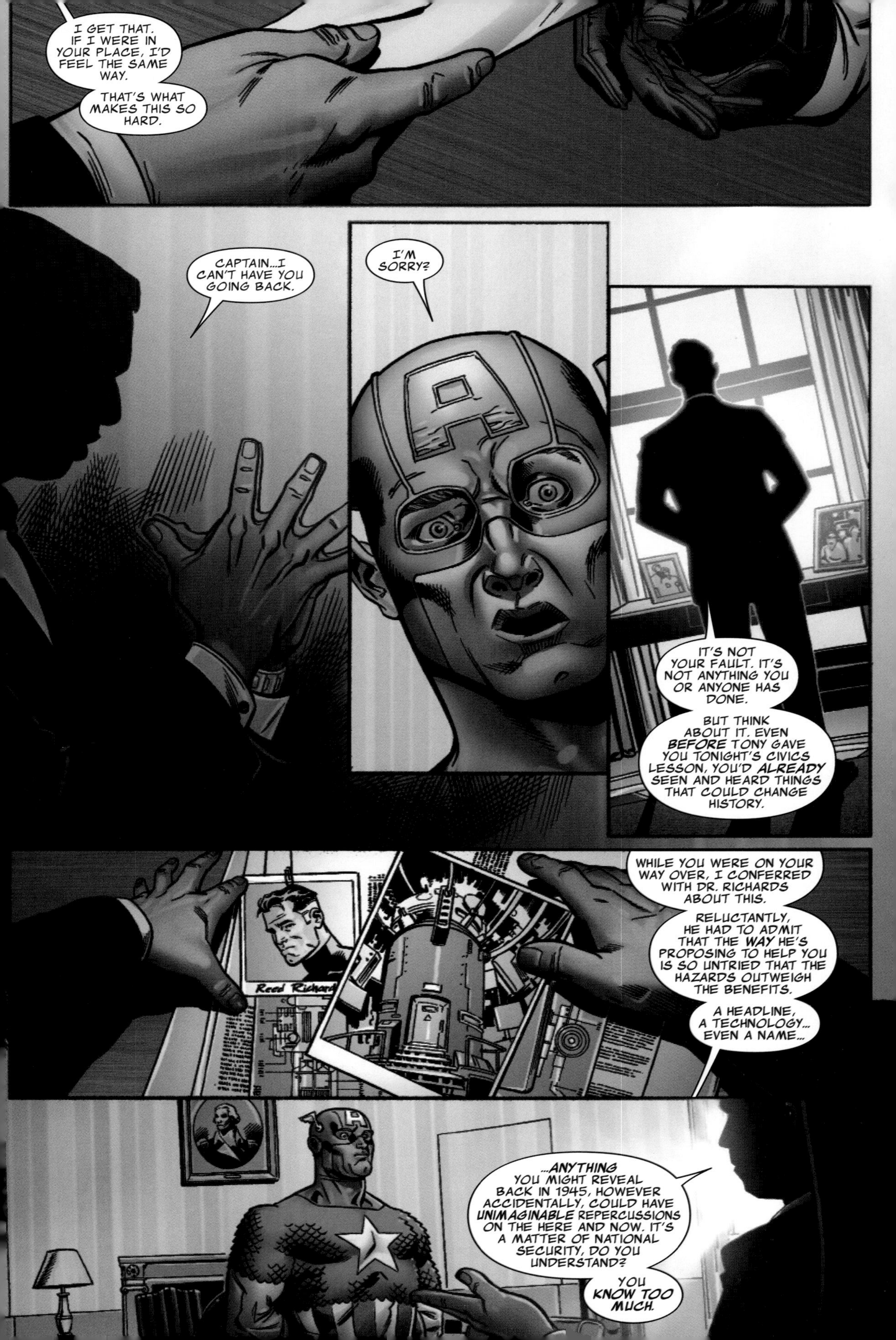
I GET THAT. IF I WERE IN YOUR PLACE, I'D FEEL THE SAME WAY.
THAT'S WHAT MAKES THIS SO HARD.
CAPTAIN...I CAN'T HAVE YOU GOING BACK.
I'M SORRY?
IT'S NOT YOUR FAULT. IT'S NOT ANYTHING YOU OR ANYONE HAS DONE.
BUT THINK ABOUT IT. EVEN BEFORE TONY GAVE YOU TONIGHT'S CIVICS LESSON, YOU'D ALREADY SEEN AND HEARD THINGS THAT COULD CHANGE HISTORY.
WHILE YOU WERE ON YOUR WAY OVER, I CONFERRED WITH DR. RICHARDS ABOUT THIS.
RELUCTANTLY, HE HAD TO ADMIT THAT THE WAY HE'S PROPOSING TO HELP YOU IS SO UNTRIED THAT THE HAZARDS OUTWEIGH THE BENEFITS.
A HEADLINE, A TECHNOLOGY... EVEN A NAME...
Reed Richards
...ANYTHING YOU MIGHT REVEAL BACK IN 1945, HOWEVER ACCIDENTALLY, COULD HAVE UNIMAGINABLE REPERCUSSIONS ON THE HERE AND NOW. IT'S A MATTER OF NATIONAL SECURITY, DO YOU UNDERSTAND?
YOU KNOW TOO MUCH.

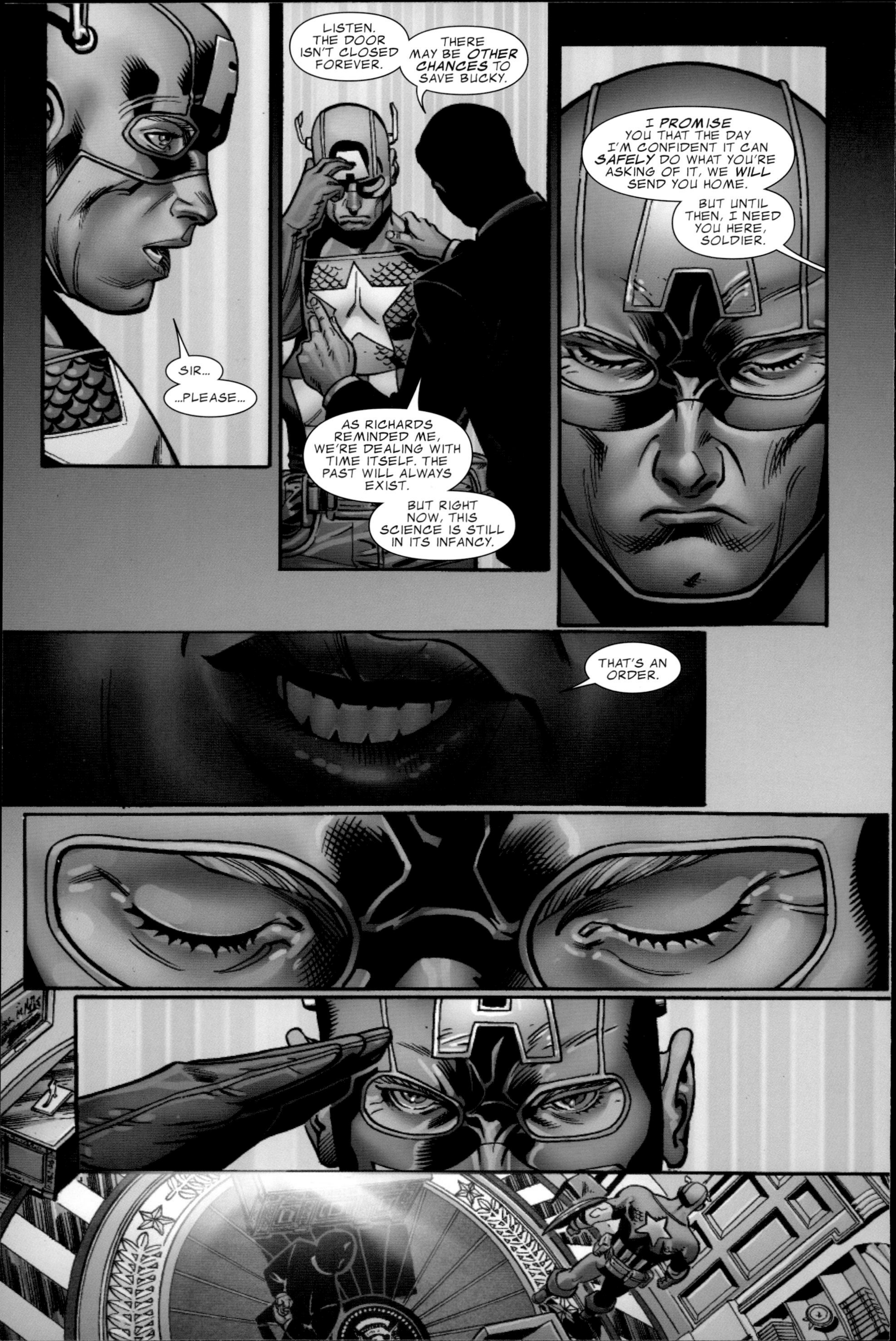
SIR...
...PLEASE...
LISTEN. THE DOOR ISN'T CLOSED FOREVER.
THERE MAY BE OTHER CHANCES TO SAVE BUCKY.
AS RICHARDS REMINDED ME, WE'RE DEALING WITH TIME ITSELF. THE PAST WILL ALWAYS EXIST.
BUT RIGHT NOW, THIS SCIENCE IS STILL IN ITS INFANCY.
I PROMISE YOU THAT THE DAY I'M CONFIDENT IT CAN SAFELY DO WHAT YOU'RE ASKING OF IT, WE WILL SEND YOU HOME.
BUT UNTIL THEN, I NEED YOU HERE, SOLDIER.
THAT'S AN ORDER.

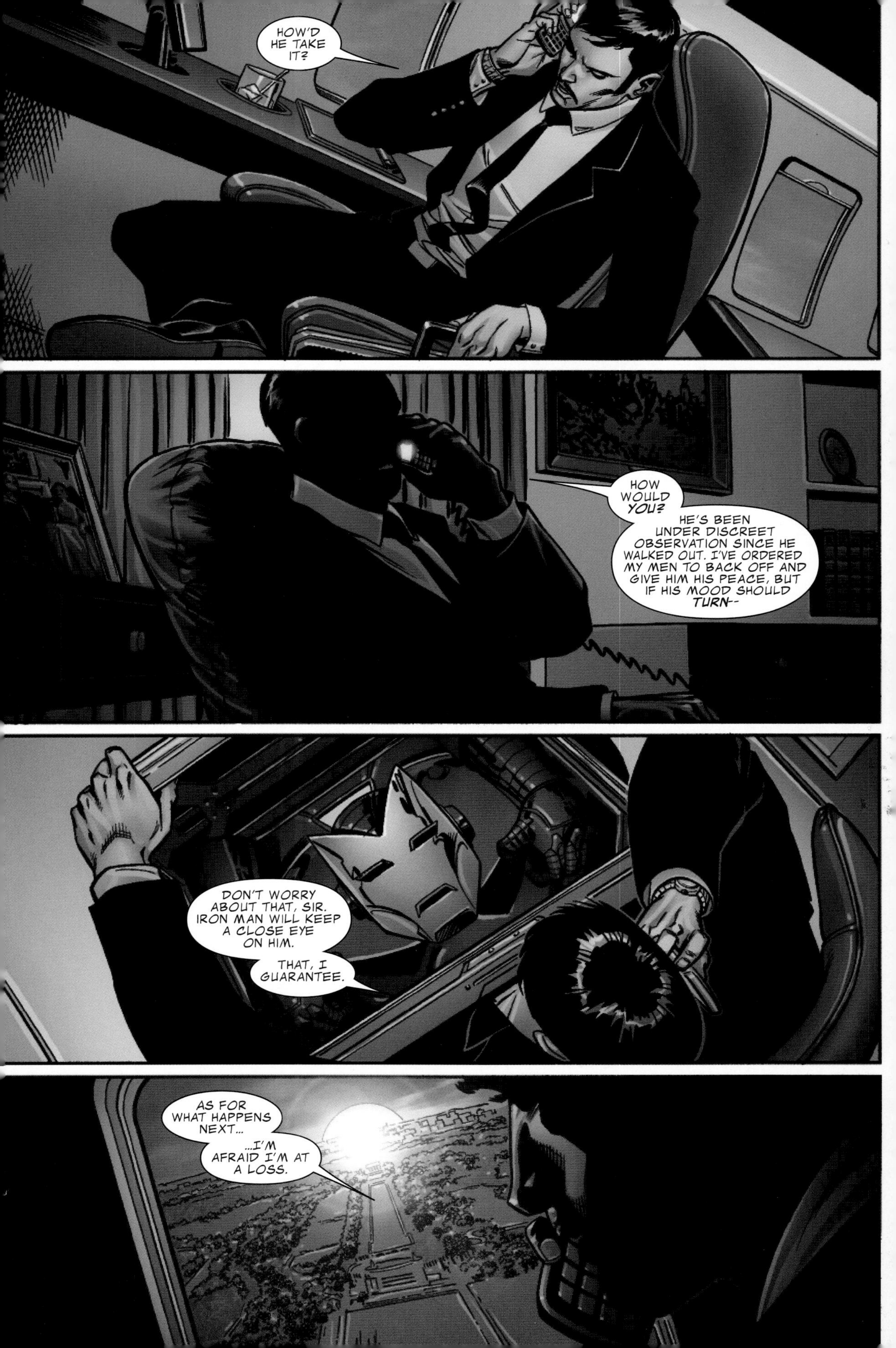

HOW'D HE TAKE IT?
HOW WOULD YOU?
HE'S BEEN UNDER DISCREET OBSERVATION SINCE HE WALKED OUT. I'VE ORDERED MY MEN TO BACK OFF AND GIVE HIM HIS PEACE, BUT IF HIS MOOD SHOULD TURN--
DON'T WORRY ABOUT THAT, SIR. IRON MAN WILL KEEP A CLOSE EYE ON HIM.
THAT, I GUARANTEE.
AS FOR WHAT HAPPENS NEXT...
...I'M AFRAID I'M AT A LOSS.

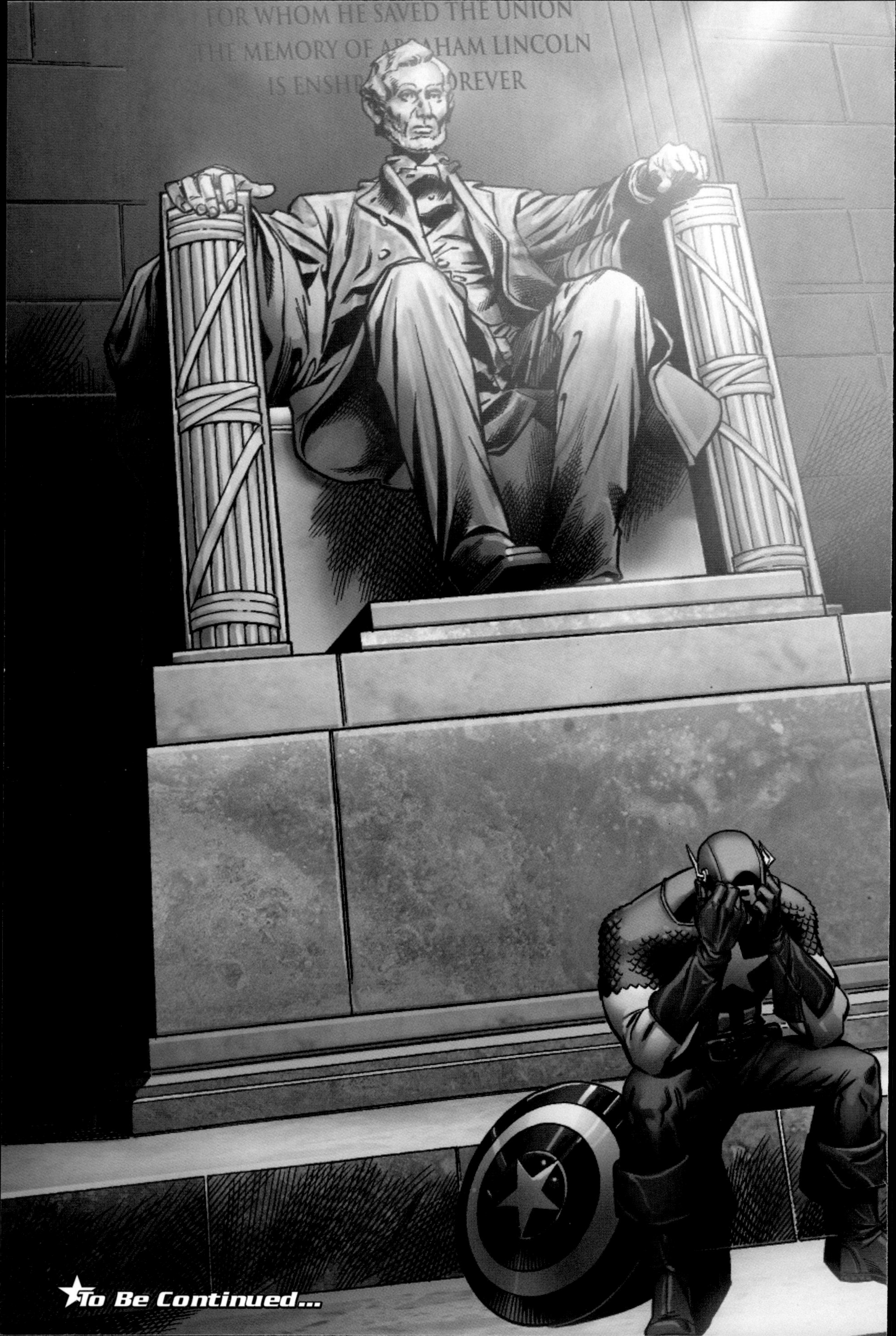
FOR WHOM HE SAVED THE UNION
To Be Continued...